This edition published by Parragon Books Ltd in 2015

Parragon Books Ltd
Chartist House
15–17 Trim Street
Bath BA1 1HA, UK
www.parragon.com

ISBN 978-1-4723-9059-2

Printed in China

# Rapunzel
## and the Jewels of the Crown

Bath · New York · Cologne · Melbourne · Delhi
Hong Kong · Shenzhen · Singapore · Amsterdam

Rapunzel is excited! With her friends' help, she has finally escaped the tower and evil Mother Gothel. Rapunzel, Flynn, Pascal and Maximus are on their way back to the kingdom. Soon, Rapunzel will meet her true parents, the King and Queen.

But Rapunzel is nervous. "Flynn, I don't think I know how to be a princess," she says.

Flynn smiles and says, "You'll be a great princess! All you have to do is wear a huge, heavy crown...."

"Oh, my!" cries Rapunzel. "Now I feel even more nervous than before!"

"Relax," Flynn says, laughing. "Do you remember the tiara from my satchel?"

Rapunzel nods.

"Well, let me tell you a little story...."

When I was a young boy, I read a book about a princess and her tiara. The book said that a tiara represented everything a princess should be.

White crystals stand for an adventurous spirit,
while green represents gentleness and kindness.
Red crystals stand for strength and courage,
and the round golden crown stands for leadership.

*I always wondered where I'd find a princess like that. Until one day, I found just the girl. She sure was adventurous!*

She showed kindness towards everyone she met.
She was brave and strong, and always knew how
to make everyone smile. She was a true princess.

"Flynn, are you talking about … " says Rapunzel.
"You!" Flynn exclaims. "I'm talking about all the
amazing things you did when you left your tower
in search of the floating lights."

"But that was when I had long, magical hair!" cries Rapunzel. "Now I just feel off-balance. I'm afraid I don't know how to help anyone without magic."

Suddenly, a group of men appears behind
Flynn and Rapunzel.

"Nobody move!" shouts one of the men.
"Give me your horse – now!"

Flynn leaps into action and chases the thieves.
"Run away, Rapunzel!" he shouts.

But Rapunzel doesn't listen. Instead, she runs right into the middle of the fighting men and rescues Maximus!

Flynn jumps onto Maximus' back to keep fighting.
But Maximus accidentally bucks him off into the water!

Finally, it's all over. Rapunzel is furious and yells at the men for fighting.

"It's all my fault," replies one man. "I need your horse to take my son to the doctor. Please, can you help me?"

"Of course! Where is he?" Rapunzel asks.
The man takes Rapunzel and her friends to
see his son. After Rapunzel tends to his injuries,
Flynn lifts the little boy on to Maximus and they
ride to see the kingdom's doctor.

"Thank you for your kindness, Rapunzel. Can you forgive us?" the men ask.

Rapunzel remembers the tiara from Flynn's story: adventure, kindness, courage and leadership.

Suddenly, she realizes she doesn't need her magical hair after all.

"A princess always forgives her friends," she says.

Rapunzel arrives at the kingdom to receive her crown. As she waves to the cheering crowd, she turns to give a special wave to her friends. After all, friends are the most precious jewels of all.

# Rapunzel's tips for being a princess

1. Be gentle and kind.

2. Treat every day like it's an adventure.

3. Don't be afraid to let your imagination run wild.

4. Always be ready to learn new things.

5. Follow your heart.

6. Smile!